3,00

D0091778

Jenny Cat-napped Cat

Written by
Celeste perrino Walker

Book 3
Created by
Jerry D. Thomas

Pacific Press Publishing Association
Boise, Idaho
Oshawa, Ontario, Canada

Edited by Jerry D. Thomas
Designed by Dennis Ferree
Cover art by Stephanie Britt
Illustrations by Mark Ford
Typeset in New Century Schoolbook 14/17

Library of Congress Cataloging-in-Publication
Data:
Walker, Celeste perrino.
    Jenny's cat-napped cat / written by Celeste perrino Walker;
[illustrated by Mark Ford] ; created by Jerry D. Thomas.
      p.   cm. — (The shoebox kids ; 3)
    Summary: Angry at the owner of a dog who has chased her
cat away, Jenny tries to track down her missing pet and, with
the help of praying to Jesus, learns about forgiveness.
    ISBN 0-8163-1277-X (alk. paper)
    [1. Cats. 2. Lost and found possessions. 3. Christian life.]
I. Ford, Mark, ill. II. Thomas, Jerry D., 1959- . III. Title. IV.
Series.
PZ7.W15226Je   1995
[Fic]—dc20   95-30634
                                         CIP
                                         AC

95 96 97 98 99 • 5 4 3 2 1

Contents

Other Books in
The Shoebox Kids Series

Hi!

Do you ever have a hard time forgiving someone who hurts you? What if they did something really bad? What if it was their fault that your best friend is gone, maybe forever?

The Shoebox Kids are back! The same kids you read about in *Primary Treasure* are in their third book. This time, when Jenny's cat, Butterscotch, runs away, Jenny knows just who to blame—she thinks. But the clues make her think again. Maybe Butterscotch didn't run away! Maybe she was cat-napped!

Jenny's Cat-napped Cat is written by my friend, Celeste Walker. She's created a story that shows you how great it is to have a pet, and how sad it can be when a pet disappears. While Jenny and her friend, Natalie, search for clues about what happened to Butterscotch, Jenny learns some important lessons about forgiveness.

Reading about Jenny and the Shoebox Kids is more than just fun—it's about learning what the Bible really means—at home, at school, or on the playground. If you're trying to be a friend of Jesus', then the Shoebox Kids books are just right for you!

Can you figure out what happened to Butterscotch before Jenny does?

Jerry D. Thomas

P.S. Book 4, *The Mystery of the Missing Combination* is coming soon!

CHAPTER 1

Butterscotch Disappears

Jenny Wallace rolled Butterscotch's beat-up old play mouse in her fingers as a tear slipped down her cheek. She missed her cat.

Three weeks ago, Butterscotch disappeared. She didn't run away—Jenny knew she would never do that. Either someone had stolen her or she was . . . Jenny couldn't even think about that.

Taking Butterscotch's mouse, Jenny walked over to the window and opened it. A little breeze tugged on her hair. She stared out into the darkness. "Come home, Butterscotch," she called softly. Somewhere out there, Butterscotch was waiting for Jenny to find her. Maybe if she waited just a little longer, Butterscotch would run up the driveway and into her arms.

Finally, she gave up and closed the window. Flopping onto her bed, she covered her face with her hands and thought back for the thousandth time. Back to when it all started, back to the day of Mrs. Shue's announcement. In her mind, it happened all over again.

"Hurry, Mom," Jenny urged her mother. She leaned forward as if she could make the car go faster.

Mrs. Wallace glanced over at the excited expression on Jenny's face. "Why are you in such a hurry this morning?" she asked with a laugh.

"Mrs. Shue said that she has a surprise for us today," Jenny explained. Then she saw a twinkle in her mother's eye.

"Hey, wait a minute. Mom, do you know what Mrs. Shue is going to tell us?" Jenny asked.

Her mother smiled. "It's no secret. At least, it won't be after today."

No matter how hard Jenny begged, her mother wouldn't give even the tiniest little hint about the "Surprise." "I don't want to spoil Mrs. Shue's announcement" was all she would say.

"Well, fine," Jenny said as she gave up. For a second, she sat with her arms folded and tried to look mad. But she was too excited to be that still. She twisted in her seatbelt and stared out the window at a big jet taking off from the airport. *I wish I was the pilot of that plane,* she thought. *I'd turn it around and head straight to the Shoebox.*

"I said, do you know your memory verse?" Jenny's mom repeated. "Jenny?"

"Huh?" Jenny jerked as she snapped back to where she really was—in the car. "My memory verse? It's, 'So in everything, do to others what you would have them do to you,' Matthew 7:12," Jenny repeated quickly.

Mrs. Wallace beamed. "I'm so proud of you, Jenny. You've learned every memory verse for this entire quarter."

Jenny squirmed as a happy flush stole over her face. Every time she learned all her memory verses, she got to choose a reward.

"Mom," she shrieked, "Stop the car!"

Mrs. Wallace pulled into a parking space. "Why?"

"Because we're here," Jenny smiled sweetly before she bolted from the car and into the church.

Before she even opened the door to the Shoebox, Jenny heard a low buzzing, as if there was a swarm of angry bees inside. Her hand felt slippery as she turned the doorknob. The buzz stopped the moment she opened the door and stepped inside. Once everyone saw it was Jenny and not Mrs. Shue, the buzz started again.

Jenny stepped quickly over to where her friend DeeDee was talking to Willie and a stranger. The tall boy had very short hair and a sour frown. He tapped one of his huge, unlaced hi-top sneakers on the floor impatiently.

"Where's Mrs. Shue?" Jenny asked in a whisper although she wasn't really sure why she was whispering in the first place.

"She's not here yet," DeeDee said, as if Jenny couldn't see that for herself.

"Jenny, this is . . ." DeeDee began. But before she could finish, Mrs. Shue opened the door and stepped inside. She smiled at them as they all found seats and looked up at her, waiting to hear what the surprise was.

"I have something to tell you all," Mrs. Shue

began breathlessly. Jenny thought she could almost feel the floor tip as everyone leaned forward to hear what Mrs. Shue had to say. "We're going to have a Family Day here at the church. It will be in the parking lot. There will be a big picnic, some fun games, displays by all the classes, and a pet show."

At the words "pet show," Jenny gasped.

"Dr. Givens, the veterinarian, will judge the pet show. A blue ribbon will be awarded to the animal that has had the best care. But the owners will also be judged—the winning pet's owner must be able to answer questions about caring for his or her pet."

"Butterscotch is going to win that blue ribbon," Jenny whispered to DeeDee, not taking her eyes off Mrs. Shue, who wasn't finished yet.

"Pastor Hill has also promised to give us a booth to run," Mrs. Shue continued. "But we have to decide what kind of booth. I thought we might want a nature display. What do you all think?"

Suggestions came from all over. It seemed like every kid in the Shoebox, except for Jenny and the stranger, had an opinion about what their display should be. Jenny was busy planning her speech for the time when she and Butterscotch would win the blue ribbon. She didn't even notice that the stranger was frowning so hard it looked as if his mouth might slide right off his face.

"OK, quiet, everyone." Mrs. Shue held up her hands. "I think the best plan is to have a nature table. Everyone be on the lookout for nature things that we can display."

After church, Jenny looked around for Maria. But she found DeeDee and the stranger.

"Jenny, I want you to meet my cousin, Tevin Ryan," DeeDee said. "He and his family will be staying with us for a few days. They're moving into a neighborhood near yours."

"Hello," Jenny said, smiling. "I didn't know DeeDee had a cousin who was our age."

"I'm not your age. I'm ten," Tevin said, tipping his nose toward the ceiling.

"Oh. Will you be going to Family Day?" Jenny asked politely, studying the bottom of Tevin's chin.

Tevin's nose dropped until it was pointing directly at Jenny. "Why would I want to go to your old Family Day? Where I'm from, we have a big fair, not some poor excuse for fun."

"I think this will be fun," Jenny said quietly, wondering to herself why Tevin was determined not to be nice. Her memory verse flashed through her mind—" So in everything, do to others what you would have them do to you."

"Why are your lips moving?" Tevin asked suddenly, looking at Jenny as if he expected her to break out in purple spots and crow like a rooster next.

"Were they?" Jenny's hand flew up to cover her mouth. "I was just remembering something."

"Well, you ought to remember it with your mouth closed or someone might think you're losing your marbles," Tevin advised. "Come on, DeeDee, let's find your parents and go. I'm starving."

DeeDee shrugged as Tevin grabbed her arm and yanked her along like a rag doll.

"Jenny," Maria's little sister Yoyo tugged on Jenny's sleeve. "I'll help you look for them."

Jenny tore her eyes from DeeDee and Tevin and looked down at Yoyo. "Help me look for what, Yoyo?" she asked.

"The marbles that boy said you lost." Yoyo said.

Jenny smiled. "He didn't really mean I had any marbles to lose," Jenny tried to explain.

"I'll give you some of my marbles," Yoyo offered. Luckily for Jenny, Maria walked up.

"Here you are, Yoyo," Maria said. "Mom is looking for you." As Yoyo skipped away, Maria turned to Jenny.

"Do you want to come eat dinner with us today? My mom said to invite you and your mother."

"Not today," Jenny replied. "We're going on a picnic and a hike to celebrate."

"Celebrate what?" Maria asked curiously.

"I won the Memory Verse Challenge last night, so Mom told me we could do something I wanted to do today."

"Well, keep your eyes open for stuff to show on our nature table," Maria said. "I can't wait for Family Day."

"Me either," Jenny answered. But she wasn't thinking of the nature table. She was thinking about Butterscotch and a blue ribbon.

2

The Blue-Ribbon Plan

Jenny's mother had her head stuck in the refrigerator while Jenny ate her breakfast. "Genuine, is this your feet putter watch?" she asked.

Jenny's hand stopped halfway to her mouth. "Huh?"

Her mother closed the door of the fridge and held out a glass bowl filled with something that smelled very strange. "I said, 'Jenny, what is this you're feeding Butterscotch?' " She tapped the bowl with one finger. "And why is it in one of my good bowls?"

17

Jenny finished another spoonful of Captain Crusader cereal before she answered. "It's a special diet, Mom. I asked the man at the pet store what would make Butterscotch's coat shine, and this is what he said to feed her."

"Couldn't you just brush her?" Mrs. Wallace asked, wrinkling her nose at the nasty smell.

"Oh, I'm doing that too," Jenny replied eagerly.

Mrs. Wallace spooned Butterscotch's food into a plastic container and put a cover on it. "Let's keep it in here when she isn't eating it," she told Jenny. "You can still use the bowl, although I can't imagine why you want to feed her out of a good glass bowl."

"So she'll feel special," Jenny explained.

Mrs. Wallace laughed. "Why don't I just get down the crystal dishes so she'll feel *really* special?"

"Would you?" Jenny asked hopefully, before she realized that her mother was joking.

As always, Jenny waited for her friend, Natalie, so they could walk to the bus stop together. Natalie had already heard about the pet show. "I brush Butterscotch every night for at least fifteen minutes," Jenny explained again.

"And she doesn't mind?" Natalie asked.

"No, Butterscotch loves to be brushed," Jenny said. "And she loves the special diet I put her on. It's making her coat really shiny. This afternoon during library time, I am going to get a book about cats from Mr. Boardman so I can study up on them."

Mr. Boardman recommended a book called *Me And My Cat.* Jenny put it in her bookbag and took it with her everywhere she went, reading it at lunch and sometimes during recess. Natalie jumped rope on the playground beside her.

"Come on, Jenny," she called. "You can read that old book anytime. Let's skip rope. If we find someone else, we can practice doubles."

Jenny looked up from her book and tried to block the sunshine with one hand. "I can't, Natalie. I only have a little time to learn everything there is to know about cats so Butterscotch can win that blue ribbon."

Natalie rolled her eyes. "That's all you ever think about anymore," she whined.

"It's not the only thing," Jenny grinned, "but if I don't learn about cats, I won't win."

"Yah, yah." Natalie's jumprope blurred with speed as she jumped hot peppers. "Well, let me know when you've learned enough."

On Thursday, Natalie and Jenny sat together on the bus as they rode home from school. "Do you want to stop off at my house and help me make room on my wall to hang Butterscotch's ribbon?" Jenny asked Natalie.

"All right," Natalie agreed. "But, after that can we play horses?"

Jenny nodded. "Would you quiz me on some cat questions first?"

Natalie groaned. "Do I have to?"

"Yes," Jenny said. "You want me and Butterscotch to win, don't you?"

"Of course I do," Natalie said. "I'm your friend, aren't I?"

When they walked into Jenny's room, Butterscotch jumped off the bed and wove in and out of their legs. "I think she wants to go out," Jenny said. "I'll be right back."

Closing the door behind Butterscotch, Jenny headed for the kitchen. "Mom, can Natalie and I have some lemonade?"

Natalie's eyes grew big when she saw the big, cold glasses of lemonade. "Thanks," she said, sipping eagerly. "I was really thirsty."

Fresh lemon pieces floated around in the

glasses, and Natalie fished for one, then bit into it and made a face. "Eeeyoo," she said. "Sour."

"Of course it's sour, silly. What do you want to do first? Ask me questions? Or make room on my wall for the ribbon?"

Natalie sat down carefully on the edge of Jenny's bed. "Questions," she said.

Jenny handed her the book and answered questions until Natalie got tired of asking them.

"Jenny," her mother said, poking her head into Jenny's bedroom. "Please be sure Butterscotch is in before it gets dark."

"Sure, Mom," Jenny said. "If we hurry," she told Natalie, "we'll just have time to make a spot on my wall for the ribbon. Then I'll go let Butterscotch in, and we'll show her."

"Don't forget you said we could play horses," Natalie reminded Jenny.

"I won't forget," Jenny promised. Climbing up on her bed, she carefully took down her cat calendar and poster of a cat that looked almost exactly like Butterscotch and handed them to Natalie. "Here. Would you put these on my dresser, please?"

Natalie placed them gently on Jenny's dresser. Jenny bounced off the bed and walked across her bedroom floor to see how the spot looked from across the room. She looked at the wall and then at Natalie who was impatiently tapping her foot.

"I just had a great idea," she said excitedly. "Why don't you come to Family Day too? Do you think you could?"

Natalie looked surprised. "I could come?"

"Sure, why don't you ask your parents?" Jenny suggested.

"All right, I will." Natalie agreed.

Jenny pointed to the wall. "What do you think?" she asked.

"I think it's a good spot." Natalie agreed. "Now can we play horses?"

Jenny laughed. "OK, now we can play horses."

They raced each other to the door. Just as Jenny reached out to open it, her mother came around the corner.

"Oh, Jenny, did you bring Butterscotch in yet?" she asked.

Jenny gulped. "No, not yet, Mom. I'll do it right now."

Mrs. Wallace nodded. "Good. We wouldn't want her to be out after dark. You never know what could happen to her."

"Hey," Natalie said as Jenny came out, "let's play hopscotch instead." By the time Jenny returned with chalk to make lines on the driveway, she had forgotten all about Butterscotch.

When Jenny got back, Natalie had found a small stone to use as a marker. "You first," she said generously.

"OK." Jenny threw the stone and started hopping. They had been playing for about fifteen minutes when a loud *toot!* made them both jump. As they stepped off onto the grass to let a big station wagon pull into the driveway, Jenny frowned. Inside the car was DeeDee's cousin Tevin.

Before Tevin or his parents could get out of the car, DeeDee and her family drove up behind them. DeeDee bounded out of the car almost before it stopped.

"Hi, Jenny!" she called. "Tevin and his family are going to move into their new house tonight, so we stopped by to visit on the way over."

Inside, Jenny groaned. She looked nervously at Natalie and wondered if, just once, Tevin could force himself to be nice.

Tevin's mother got out of the car talking so

fast that Jenny wondered how she managed to breathe.

"You'd better get out and take advantage of the chance to rest, Tevin, because you'll get awfully tired unpacking your things and getting your room straightened out once we get home. I won't have a moment's peace until we get everything organized. Boxes, boxes, everywhere." She turned around before she had walked halfway up the driveway to the house. "Tevin? Get out and visit."

When Tevin stuck his legs out of the door, his mother turned around and kept walking toward the house with Tevin's father and Mr. and Mrs. Adams. Before he got out, Tevin pushed back a little brown-and-white dog that was trying to scramble over his lap and get out of the door.

"Stay here, Shorty," he said gruffly as he got out and slammed the door behind him.

"That's a cute dog," Jenny offered, as she watched the little creature scratch excitedly on the car window. Suddenly, the dog started bouncing up and down like a basketball.

Tevin glanced at the dog. "He's OK for a dog, I guess."

"Don't you like dogs?" Natalie asked, but before Tevin could answer, Natalie's mother called her from down the street. She turned to Jenny. "Sorry, guess I've got to go."

"I'll see you later," Jenny called as she watched Natalie jog toward home.

"Tevin," his mother shrieked, sticking her head out the front door. "Let Shorty out to do his business."

"Yes, Mom," Tevin said, opening the door of the car. The little dog shot out from inside the car as if he'd been fired from a cannon. Jenny giggled at him as he darted around the yard sniffing everything.

"He's so short. He looks like a beagle that got cut off at the knees," she said.

"I don't like dogs," Tevin replied sourly.

"Why not?" DeeDee asked.

Tevin shrugged. "I just don't. I only like cats."

"Do you have any cats?" Jenny asked.

"No," Tevin replied, "but I'm going to get one real soon."

"Can we go inside?" DeeDee asked suddenly. "I'm getting chilly out here."

Before they made it to the front steps, Tevin remembered that Shorty was still running around the yard. He turned back just as a horrible squeal stopped them all in their tracks.

"What was that?" Jenny asked. At the same moment, she had an awful feeling that she knew what it was. "Butterscotch!" she wailed.

3

Shorty and Butterscotch

"Butterscotch!"

A golden shape hurtled across the yard, followed by a brown-and-white barking blur. Butterscotch disappeared behind the cars parked in the driveway with Shorty right behind her. Jenny was across the lawn before she even realized that her legs had moved.

"Butterscotch, come back!" she shouted. "Butterscotch!" But as she strained to see down the street, a bulky white truck roared by. "Stop!" she shouted. But the truck kept going. Somewhere ahead of it, she could still hear Shorty's sharp barking. "Oh no!" she wailed.

Near the next cross street, the truck's red brake lights lit up. Tires squealed as it slammed to a stop. Jenny's hand covered her eyes. DeeDee covered her ears. Tevin just stared.

"Oh no, oh no," Jenny said as she peeked through her fingers. She watched the truck door open and the driver hop out. As the man walked around in front of his truck, Jenny turned and grabbed DeeDee.

"Come on! Butterscotch might be hurt. Tevin, go get my mom—and yours. Shorty might be hurt too!" Tevin frowned and turned toward the door.

As Jenny whirled back toward the street, she heard the door of the truck slam closed. "Hey—hey, wait!" she shouted as she and DeeDee ran. But the truck rolled away. Jenny raced up to the spot where it had stopped—and froze—afraid to look down.

"I don't see anything," DeeDee said. "Butterscotch? Shorty?" There was no bark or meow for an answer. "Jenny, I don't think they're here."

Jenny dared to look around. She didn't see any broken animal bodies or blood. "Butterscotch," she called. "Come here, girl."

By that time, Mrs. Wallace ran up. DeeDee's dad and her uncle were right behind her. "Do you see her?" Mrs. Wallace asked, breathing hard. "Is she hurt?"

"I don't see her at all," Jenny wailed.

"Where's Shorty?" Tevin called from down the street. He was walking slowly toward them.

"We haven't seen him," DeeDee answered.

Tevin's dad pulled a flashlight out of his pocket and walked along the edge of the street looking into each yard. "They could have been hurt," he said quietly. Then louder, he called, "Shorty! Biscuit!"

"Who's Biscuit?" DeeDee asked.

Her uncle pulled out a dog biscuit. "He always comes for a biscuit. He must not be nearby."

"I don't think Butterscotch is near either," Jenny's mom said. "I'm sorry, dear."

Jenny wiped off a tear. "She could be scared and hiding." Then she got mad. "It's that dog's fault! He chased her away!"

"Now, Jenny," her mother said, laying a hand on her shoulder. "Dogs do chase cats. That's just the way it is. You know that's why Butterscotch usually stays in the house."

Jenny didn't answer her. She was too busy

thinking bad thoughts about Shorty. *But, it wasn't really Shorty's fault, like Mom said,* she thought and looked straight at Tevin. *It's Tevin's fault!*

Then she glared at DeeDee. DeeDee was staring off into the darkness as if looking really hard would make Butterscotch appear. *And it's DeeDee's fault because Tevin is her cousin. If it wasn't for DeeDee, then Tevin wouldn't be here; and if Tevin wasn't here, then his old dog couldn't have chased Butterscotch away in the first place.*

"I'm sure Butterscotch will head for home, sweetheart," her mother said. "Let's do the same thing. We can't make her come back by standing around in the street." She smiled at Jenny, but Jenny couldn't smile back.

Tevin's dad walked down the street calling Shorty and waving a biscuit. As they walked across the yard, Tevin's mother scolded him. "Tevin, why did you leave the car door open? Shut it right now, please."

Jenny followed everyone into the house, but when they sat down to talk, she went to her room and pretended to read a book. Really, she just lay on her bed and stared at the pages.

Without thinking, she reached out her hand

to where Butterscotch was usually curled up against her leg. But instead of the warm fur of her pet, her fingers brushed the fake fur of her stuffed grizzly bear. Angrily, she tossed it onto the floor.

Gulping back a sniffle, Jenny rolled over and stared at the ceiling. She didn't feel like visiting. She didn't feel like reading. She didn't feel like doing anything until Butterscotch came back.

"Jenny?" her mother said softly, opening the door enough to stick her head in. "DeeDee and Tevin are leaving. Why don't you come out and say goodbye?"

Jenny pushed herself off the bed slowly. She would go out because her mother asked her to, but she wouldn't say goodbye.

"Bye, Jenny," DeeDee said as she left. She looked puzzled when Jenny just stood there and didn't say anything back.

"We'll keep looking for Shorty," Mrs. Wallace called to Tevin's dad. "He'll show up before long."

I'm not looking for Shorty, Jenny promised herself as she changed into her pajamas and crawled into bed. *I hope no one ever sees him again. Shorty deserves to be lost, but Butter-scotch doesn't!*

It was a long time before Jenny fell asleep. And by then, her pillow was wet with tears.

4

Looking for Clues

By Monday morning, Butterscotch still hadn't come home. As far as they were able to tell, ncither had Shorty.

Jenny watched her mom sadly spoon Butterscotch's special diet into the trash because it was starting to stink up the refrigerator. Her eyes wandered over to the shelf where she kept Butterscotch's brush. There were a few cat hairs stuck in the bristles, but she didn't want to clean it out. Right now, that fur was all she had left of Butterscotch.

"Are you going to eat that?" Natalie asked at

lunch time.

"Huh?" Jenny said.

"Your apple? Are you going to eat it?"

Jenny sighed. "No. You can have it." Food just didn't taste good anymore.

Natalie took the apple and bit into it with a big *Crunch!* "Thish ish a good apple," she said, trying to talk around the big bite. She chewed for a while, then set the apple down. "Aren't you ever going to smile again?"

Jenny shrugged her shoulders. "I don't know. Maybe someday when I grow up."

"I have an idea!" Natalie said. "Why don't we search around your house for clues. We can find Butterscotch. I know we can."

Jenny brightened a little. "Do you think so?" she asked hopefully.

Natalie thumped Jenny on the back. "Sure we can. I'll meet you at your house after school tonight. OK?"

Jenny nodded. "OK."

That afternoon she waited impatiently at the end of her driveway for Natalie to change her clothes and meet her. Finally, just when Jenny was about to go look for her, Natalie burst out of her front door and ran over.

"Sorry," she panted breathlessly. "My mom wanted me to help her fold some clothes before I left."

She searched her pockets for something. "But, look what my dad let us borrow," she continued, pulling a big magnifying glass out of her pocket.

She held it up to her eye. Jenny jumped. The magnifying glass made Natalie's eye look huge. The giant eye blinked at her. "What do you think?" Natalie asked.

"Wow," Jenny said. "What do we do with it?"

"Look for clues, of course," Natalie replied. She began looking carefully at the grass around the driveway. "Didn't you say that Butterscotch ran across the lawn and then down the road?"

Jenny nodded. "Yes," she thought back to the awful night. "I heard this horrible squeal, and then I saw Butterscotch run across the yard with Shorty right behind her. They ran behind the cars and then down the street." She fought back tears. "Then that truck roared by. When it squealed to a stop, I just knew she was going to be hit."

Natalie pretended she didn't notice that Jenny was almost crying. "But she wasn't, right?

At least, you didn't find her on the street. Come on, I think we should start here."

Jenny followed along behind Natalie, who was crawling through the grass on the lawn toward the driveway. She pushed the grass to the side trying to see little cat prints in the dirt. Suddenly, Natalie stopped. She held the magnifying glass almost on the dirt.

"Ah hah!" she said. "Look at this."

Jenny crawled up beside her. "Cat prints!" she said excitedly.

"What did I tell you?" Natalie said happily. She examined the prints closely. "It almost looks like she was jumping toward the driveway."

"But, how do we know that Butterscotch made these prints that night and not some other time?" Jenny asked. "She loves chasing grasshoppers. Maybe she was jumping after one of them."

"I don't know," Natalie admitted. "But, we know she made these prints *sometime*."

Jenny sat back in the grass and tried not to look unhappy. "How are we ever going to find Butterscotch this way?"

Natalie sighed and plopped down beside her.

"I don't know. But we aren't going to find her by moping around in your room."

"Jenny!" Mrs. Wallace called. "Would you come here a minute?"

Jenny trotted to the house. Her mother handed her a stack of papers and some thumb tacks. "Here, honey, I made some posters saying that Butterscotch is missing and where to call if someone finds her. Why don't you go put them up around the neighborhood?"

Jenny threw her arms around her mother. "Thanks, Mom," she said. Then she turned. "Come on, Natalie! Mom had a great idea!"

They circled slowly around the block. "Did anyone have a reason to steal Butterscotch?" Natalie asked as she pushed a tack into a sign on a telephone pole.

"I don't think so," Jenny replied, counting out the number of posters they had left. She pointed to the next pole. "Let's put one over there." But before she had taken two steps, a thought hit her.

"Wait!" she said suddenly, stopping so fast that Natalie ran into her with a little grunt. "When that truck stopped, the driver got out and ran around to the front. I thought he was just making sure that he hadn't hit Butterscotch or Shorty. But what if he stole them?"

Natalie's eyes got big. "He could have! What kind of truck was it?"

Just then a voice interrupted them. "Excuse me, girls." It was Mrs. Morton, a woman who lived a few houses down the street. "Are you looking for your pet?"

Jenny and Natalie ran eagerly to where Mrs. Norton was working in her yard. "Yes, yes," they said together. "She's a gold colored cat named Butterscotch. Did you see her?"

"No," Mrs. Norton said slowly. "Not a cat. But Friday night, just as it was getting dark, I saw a little brown-and-white dog running down the street barking his head off."

Jenny felt her bottom lip quiver. "That was Shorty. He chased Butterscotch away."

"Did you see a big truck about the same time?" Natalie asked.

"Yes," Mrs. Norton said slowly. "A big yellow one. It didn't hit your pet, did it?"

"No," Jenny said. "But we haven't seen my cat since then."

"I'm sorry," Mrs. Norton said kindly. "I didn't even see a cat. Just the dog."

"Thank you anyway," Jenny forced herself to say before Natalie tugged on her arm.

"Come on, Jenny," she said. "Let's go put up the rest of these posters. Someone must have seen Butterscotch."

By the time they finished putting up posters around the neighborhood, it was time for supper. Jenny said goodbye to Natalie and walked home slowly. Her mother called to her through the kitchen window.

"No luck, huh? Well, cheer up, sweetheart. Maybe someone will recognize her from the poster and call. And I put an ad in the paper today saying that she was missing."

Jenny brightened. "You did?"

Her mom nodded. "Yes, I did. Oh, and Jenny, have you prayed about Butterscotch yet?"

"Yes," Jenny said. "But we could pray again." Her mother knelt down on the kitchen floor, and Jenny knelt down beside her.

"Dear Heavenly Father," her mother prayed. "We know that You care for all your creatures. Please be with Butterscotch wherever she is. Keep her safe, and help her to find her way home if it's Your will. Amen."

Jenny stood up and hugged her mom. God

was watching over Butterscotch. He would take care of her. Suddenly she was hungry. "Thanks, Mom. What are we having for supper? I'm starved."

Her mom leaned over the oven. "We're having gravy and biscuits."

Jenny didn't hear her. "Gravy and what?"

"Biscuits," Mom said in a loud voice. Then a voice answered her from outside the window.

"Arf! Arf!"

Jenny froze. "Oh no!"

5

The Unforgiving Servant

"Arf, arf!"

Mrs. Wallace looked puzzled. Then her eyes got big. "You don't think that's Shorty, do you?"

Jenny raced to the door. "It is Shorty! Shorty, what did you do with my cat?" Shorty didn't answer. He just danced around wagging his tail.

"Well, there you are, Shorty," Mrs. Wallace said. "Jenny, get him some of Butterscotch's food to eat. I'll call DeeDee's mom."

Jenny was horrified. "Mom! I'm not feeding him Butterscotch's food! It's his fault Butterscotch is gone!"

"Jenny, you can't blame a dog for acting like a dog. It wasn't his fault."

Jenny dug in the cupboard for some of her cat's old food. "If it isn't Shorty's fault," she muttered, "then it's Tevin's fault. Shorty is his dog." She dumped the food into a dish. "And it's DeeDee's fault, because she brought him to our house."

No one answered at DeeDee's house, so Mrs. Wallace made Jenny lock Shorty in the garage. "We'll take him to Tevin's tomorrow after church."

Jenny waited at her window all evening. *Maybe Butterscotch has been hiding from Shorty. Maybe she'll come home now.* But Butterscotch never appeared. The next morning, Jenny got ready slowly and grumpily.

"Let's get in the car," her mom called. "It's time to go."

Jenny gave her hair a quick brush and headed for the door. Today, it didn't matter what she looked like. She just didn't care. Slumped in the corner of her side of the car, she listened while her mother was talking.

"These people have no home, no nice clothes, nothing," Mrs. Wallace said. "They need help."

I need help, Jenny thought. *I need help finding my cat. I wonder if anyone cares about that. Butterscotch always listened to my problems without complaining or getting bored.* Suddenly, Jenny missed her cat more that ever. And the more she thought about it, the more she missed her until finally tears started to trickle down her cheek. She wiped them carefully away so her mother wouldn't see them and ask why she was crying.

Jenny slunk into the Shoebox as if she was trying to hide, but Maria pounced on her the way Butterscotch used to pounce on grasshoppers.

"Jenny, sit next to me, OK?" Maria asked.

"All right," Jenny agreed. She followed Maria and sat beside her. She was careful not to look at DeeDee and so she missed the hurt look on DeeDee's face.

"I'm so excited, aren't you excited?" Maria said. "I can't wait for Family Day."

"I can," Jenny muttered.

Maria looked surprised. "You can? Why? Before, you couldn't stop talking about it."

"That was before Butterscotch disappeared," Jenny said, trying hard not to cry again.

Maria's eyes opened wide in surprise. "Your beautiful cat disappeared? How? Did someone cat-nap her?"

Jenny shot a mean look toward DeeDee. "No, it was DeeDee's fault. Her cousin's dog chased Butterscotch away. Now we won't be able to be in the pet show on Family Day. I . . . I don't even think I want to go at all now."

"You can't mean that," Maria said.

Jenny stuck her chin out stubbornly. "I do. I do mean it."

Before Maria could say anything else, Mrs. Shue came in the room, and everyone settled down. Mrs. Shue smiled brightly at them.

"We're going to do a little play-acting this morning. Can I have some volunteers?" Several hands went up, and Mrs. Shue chose Sammy and DeeDee. Then everyone's hands went down, and they sat back to see what was going to happen.

"Oops," Mrs. Shue said. "I need three volunteers. Jenny? Would you come up and be our third person?"

Jenny tried not to groan. She hadn't even had her hand up to be picked in the first place. Besides, DeeDee was up there, and she wasn't even sure she could speak to DeeDee after what happened. Still, she couldn't disappoint Mrs. Shue.

"Yes," she said, walking as slowly as she could to the front of the room. DeeDee gave her a puzzled look but didn't say anything. Mrs. Shue handed them each a piece of paper with their lines on it.

"Sammy, you're the king," she said. "And Jenny, you're the first servant. DeeDee, you play the second servant. Go ahead, Sammy."

Sammy cleared his throat, and in his deepest voice, he read his lines. "I'm the king, and I'm going to settle my accounts. Bring me the man who owes me a bazillion dollars, because I'm going to sell everything he has to pay his debt." Then he frowned. "Mrs. Shue, what's a bazillion?"

"Lots and lots," Mrs. Shue replied. "Now, Jenny, you read your lines."

"Oh no." Jenny read flatly. "I don't have a bazillion dollars. But, if you'll be patient, I'll pay you everything."

"OK," Sammy shrugged. "Forget about it. You don't owe me a penny anymore."

For a second, everyone just stood there. Then

Mrs. Shue whispered, "Jenny, your turn."

Jenny looked at her card and saw that she was supposed to grab DeeDee by her collar and say her lines. She grabbed her shoulder instead and shook her a little harder than she needed to. "You owe me a dollar, pay up!"

DeeDee pulled away from Jenny and rubbed her shoulder. "I don't have a dollar. But, if you'll be patient with me, I'll pay you everything."

"No way," Jenny said. "Throw her in jail until she pays up."

"Sammy, would you read the ending?" Mrs. Shue asked.

"The master called the wicked servant and said, "I forgave you a bazillion dollars because you asked me to. Shouldn't you also forgive your fellow servant who owed you a dollar? I am sending you to prison until you pay every cent."

"Can anyone tell me what this lesson means?" Mrs. Shue asked the kids.

Jenny thought for a minute. Something about that story sounded very familiar. Something sounded a lot like her.

Willie raised his hand. "Is it that we need to forgive other people their sins because Jesus forgave us our sins?" he asked.

"That's exactly it," Mrs. Shue exclaimed. "The bazillion dollars, the big debt, is our sins. The dollar, the little debt, is other people's sins against us. If Jesus forgave us so much, how can we not forgive others?"

Jenny sat down in her seat slowly. She knew what she had to do, but she was scared to do it. As soon as Sabbath School was over, she made her way over to DeeDee's chair. DeeDee was gathering up her things to leave.

Jenny cleared her throat. "DeeDee? I want to tell you that I'm sorry."

DeeDee looked up. "I noticed that you haven't talked to me all week."

"I'm really sorry," Jenny said softly. "I blamed you for Butterscotch disappearing because Tevin is your cousin and Shorty is his dog. I know it wasn't your fault. Will you forgive me?"

DeeDee nodded. "Yes, I do. But, I'm awful sorry Butterscotch didn't come back."

"Oh, by the way, Shorty came back. He showed up last night when we were having biscuits for supper."

"Really!" DeeDee got excited. "I can't wait to tell Tevin." She ran off to find her mother.

Jenny thought as she walked up the stairs to

the sanctuary. *Maybe Jesus will let Butterscotch come home now that I've apologized to DeeDee. Maybe that's what He was waiting for.*

6

The Invisible Cat

"Now, behave yourself, Shorty," Mrs. Wallace said as she opened the car door. "Jenny, hold onto his leash."

Jenny held on as they walked toward the door of the Ryan's house. Tevin yanked the door open as they got near.

"So there you are, Shorty," he said. Shorty went crazy. He jumped up and barked and almost strangled himself on the leash. Finally, he jerked loose and ran into the house, barking at the top of his lungs.

"Looks like he's happy to be home," Tevin's

dad called from inside. "Thanks for bringing him back. Did you ever find the cat?"

"No," Mrs. Wallace answered. "But we haven't given up hope." As she spoke, Shorty raced back out the door and around the house. "I guess we'd better go. See you later!"

"Dumb dog," Jenny mumbled as they walked to the car. "He just got home, now he's going to get lost again." As they drove away, Jenny saw Shorty scratching at the door of an old shed that stood in the backyard. "Dumb dog," she said again. "It's not fair that they get Shorty back and Butterscotch is still gone."

The next day after school, Jenny set her books on the desk in her room. The empty spot on the wall where she was going to hang Butterscotch's blue ribbon caught her eye. She stared at it for a few minutes. *Maybe I should just put the calendar and poster back up,* she thought. *Maybe I should just give up.*

Then she shook her head. *No! I'm not giving up. There's still time for Butterscotch to come back before Family Day and win the blue ribbon.*

Jenny heard a knock on the front door, followed by the sound of her mother's voice. "Jenny, Natalie's here."

Natalie? What is she doing here? "Hi, I didn't know you were coming over."

"I had an idea when I got home. I wrote out all the clues that we found about Butterscotch. Let's pretend we're real detectives and see if we can figure out what happened to her."

Jenny shrugged. "OK." Both girls stared at the paper Natalie held. The first thing Natalie had written was:

1. Cat tracks jumping toward driveway.

"But, we don't really know if that's a clue," Jenny pointed out. "She could have been chasing grasshoppers."

The next clue was:

2. Mrs. Norton saw Shorty but not Butterscotch.

"Maybe Mrs. Norton didn't have her glasses on," Jenny suggested. "Or maybe she just can't see in the dark."

"Then how did she see Shorty?" Natalie demanded. "And what about number 3?"

3. A big yellow truck almost hit the animals. The driver got out, then got in and drove away without speaking to anyone.

"The driver could have just stopped to be sure the animals weren't hurt," Jenny pointed out.

"Then why did he or she drive away so fast?" Natalie asked. Jenny didn't have an answer. They looked at the next clue.

4. Butterscotch has not been seen around the neighborhood.

"So what does that mean?" Jenny asked.

"That maybe the truck driver took her away. Don't you think she'd come back if she was around here?"

"Well . . . yes, if she could," Jenny admitted.

"So the driver must have taken her."

Natalie had another question. "Why would the driver take Butterscotch and not take Shorty?"

"Oh, please," Jenny snorted. "Butterscotch is a beautiful creature. Shorty is just a . . . dog. So how do we find that truck?"

Natalie shrugged. "It's out there somewhere. Let's go walk around and look for it." After telling Jenny's mom, the girls headed down the street.

"Wait," Jenny said as they came to a corner. "This is where Butterscotch was running when the truck stopped."

"Are there skid marks in the street?" Natalie asked. Both girls looked both ways, then walked out past the stop sign. Natalie pointed to a pair of short black ribbons on the street. "Those must be them."

"Let me show you what happened," Jenny said. "I could see Shorty running down the sidewalk over here." She moved to that side of the intersection. "Then just as the truck came roaring up, Shorty dashed out—like this." Jenny rushed to the middle of the street. "Then the truck—"

Screech! Jenny and Natalie jumped at the sound of tires skidding behind them. Jenny spun around to see—a big yellow truck!

A woman stuck her head out of the open window on the driver's side. "Are you girls crazy? Get out of the street before someone runs over you!"

Natalie grabbed Jenny's arm. "That's her," she said. "That's the truck!"

Jenny stepped over to the driver's side. "I'm very sorry," she said. "We were trying to figure out what happened to my cat. A dog chased her down this street last week, and a big yellow truck like yours almost hit her."

The driver frowned. "You say this was a cat?"

"A golden cat," Jenny added. "Did you see it?"

The driver shook her head. "I almost hit a little dog here last week. The crazy thing ran right out in front of me—like you just did. I stopped to see if I had hit it, but it was gone."

Jenny nodded excitedly. "But what about the cat? What happened to the cat?"

"I didn't see any cat," the driver said. "Just that dog. And I hope I don't see it again. I have to go—good luck with the cat."

As the truck rumbled away, Jenny slumped down to the sidewalk. "Another dead end," she moaned. "Now we'll never find Butterscotch."

But Natalie just stood there and smiled. "Wait a minute," she said, "I don't think that was a dead end at all."

Jenny looked up. "What are you talking about? She didn't even see Butterscotch. All she saw was that dumb dog Shorty."

"Exactly," Natalie said. "Remember, that's the same thing Mrs. Norton said. She saw a dog, but not a cat."

Jenny stomped her foot. "Butterscotch isn't invisible. Why didn't anyone see her?

"What if she didn't run down the street?"

Now Jenny was really confused. "Then what did she do?"

Natalie smiled. "Let's go back to the scene of the crime."

7

Catching the Cat-napper

Standing back in her yard, Jenny stared at Natalie. "OK, we're back where it all started. What happened to my cat?"

Natalie stood at the edge of the driveway. "When did you see Butterscotch last?"

"I told you already. She raced across the yard and Shorty chased her down the street."

Natalie tilted her head. "Did you see your cat run down the street?"

Jenny closed her eyes, trying to remember exactly. "No. I saw her run across the yard toward the cars. Shorty was right behind her, so when he ran out the other side, I thought she did too."

"Everyone thought that," Natalie said, "but no one saw her. Not you, not the truck driver, not Mrs. Norton."

"But if she didn't go down the street, where did she go?"

Natalie shrugged. "What if she hid under the car, then Tevin stole her?"

Jenny thought again. "He went inside to get Mom while DeeDee and I ran down the street. I guess he could have put Butterscotch in their car before he followed everyone else to look for Shorty." Then she remembered. "No, he couldn't have. Their car door was still open when we came back. His mother yelled at him for leaving it open."

Natalie stared at Jenny. "Are you saying that the car door was open when Butterscotch ran across the yard?

Jenny's eyes got big. "The catprints! Butterscotch was jumping toward the car. What if she jumped in the car?" Then she frowned. "But, why hasn't Tevin called to tell me that he has Butterscotch. If Butterscotch jumped in his car, then it was an accident."

"You said he wanted a cat. Maybe he decided to keep her," Natalie suggested. "Didn't you say they moved in around here somewhere?"

"Yes," Jenny replied slowly.

"Do you think you could figure out a way to get over there and check?"

"Maybe I can think of something," Jenny said. By dinnertime, she had.

"Mom?" Jenny began innocently as she helped her mother peel carrots. "Don't you think it would be nice to go visit Tevin and his family soon? After all, they just moved in. We should welcome them. We could bring them a loaf of your bread."

Jenny's mom raised her eyebrows, but she agreed. "Yes, that would be a nice thing to do. What made you think of Tevin all of a sudden?"

Jenny shrugged uncomfortably. "Well, Natalie and I were looking for clues about Butterscotch, and I wanted to talk to him about it. Could we ask DeeDee to go with us? Sometimes, Tevin makes me nervous."

DeeDee was delighted to go with them. All the way to Tevin's house, she talked nonstop. Jenny tried to nod and say "uh-huh" in the right places, but she wasn't really listening. *What if*

Butterscotch is there? Oh, I hope she is!

Shorty greeted them at the door, but Tevin wasn't home. When Mrs. Wallace sat down to visit, DeeDee said, "I brought the cassette Tevin wanted, Aunt Denice. I'm just going to put it in his room."

"Be careful," her aunt answered. "His room is a disaster area. I don't want anyone getting hurt."

Jenny tagged along, glad for an excuse to check out Tevin's room. She pushed past DeeDee and got there first. "What a mess!" she said, shaking her head as she walked around the room. She didn't see anything that could belong to a cat.

"What are you doing anyway?" DeeDee asked suspiciously as Jenny went to the window and looked out. Just behind the house was the small shed Shorty had been scratching the day they brought him home. *Wait a minute,* she thought. *Maybe there's a reason why Shorty went right to that shed and wanted in.* "DeeDee, let's go outside."

"Why? What are you looking for?" DeeDee demanded.

"Something that might be in that shed,"

Jenny replied, already on her way out of the house.

"Tell me what you're doing," DeeDee said in a panicked whisper, racing after her. "Or else I'm telling your mom."

Jenny whirled around. "I think Tevin has my cat. And I think she might be in that shed. So I'm going to look. I have to."

DeeDee just stared, her eyes wide and frightened. "No way. He wouldn't do that. Would he?"

"There's only one way to find out." Jenny slipped the metal door of the shed open and stepped inside. It took a moment for her eyes to adjust to the dim lighting. Finally, objects began to come into focus.

There was a lawnmower, some garden tools, and three bicycles. She felt disappointment choke up in her throat. And then she spotted it. A stuffed mouse, the kind cats played with, lying outside of a mound covered with an old blanket. "Butterscotch?" she whispered.

Jenny could feel her heart hammering in her chest as she pulled the edge of the blanket. As it slipped off, a strong hand grasped her other arm.

"What are you doing?" a deep voice growled.

Jenny screamed as loud and long as she could before a hand clamped down over her mouth. Tevin stuck his face right in front of hers and frowned angrily at her.

"Stop it before they hear you inside," he hissed, pulling the blanket back up to cover what was under it, but not before Jenny had a chance to see what had been hidden. A rough homemade cage, bowls for food and water, and some cat toys.

"What's going on here," Tevin's mother demanded, yanking open the door of the shed. Jenny's mom peered in anxiously after her.

"Jenny? Honey? Are you hurt?"

Jenny pulled free of Tevin's grasp, tears spilling down her cheeks. "Mom! Mom! He stole Butterscotch! Tevin stole Butterscotch!"

"I did not," Tevin snapped.

Jenny's mom made her way into the crowded shed and put a hand on Jenny's shoulder. "Sweetheart, I know you miss Butterscotch, but why would you accuse Tevin of stealing her? You know that isn't true."

"Then what is this for?" Jenny asked, pulling the blanket off the cage before Tevin could stop her. His smug look melted.

"Tevin?" His mother worked her way into the shed with them. "What is that for?"

"So I had your old cat," Tevin admitted sourly. "But, I didn't steal her. She was in our car when we left. I just kept her for a while."

Jenny's voice shook when she spoke. "What do you mean 'for a while'? Where is she now?"

CHAPTER 8

Found! And Lost Again

"Where is Butterscotch?" Jenny shouted.

"I don't know," Tevin said miserably. "She ran away. I only meant to keep her for a little while. I was going to give her back." Tevin's eyes weren't angry anymore. They were sad and frightened. "I'm sorry."

Jenny heard her own voice, but couldn't believe what she was saying. " I forgive you," she managed to get out before her lips clamped shut.

The ride home was filled with silence broken only by Jenny's sobs. After they dropped DeeDee off at her house, Mom laid a hand on Jenny's knee.

"Honey," her mother said gently, "I really think you should prepare yourself to accept the fact that Butterscotch may never come home."

Jenny gulped back a big sniffle. "I know Mom, but I'm going to keep hoping."

"I know it's a little soon, but would you like to think about getting a kitten?"

Jenny shook her head fiercely. "No, I don't want another kitten. I want Butterscotch. No other cat could take her place."

"I understand, honey. We'll keep praying that Butterscotch comes home." When they got home, Jenny sank down on the couch. Her mom sat next to her and stroked Jenny's hair, just as she did whenever Jenny was sick.

I wish I was sick, Jenny thought. *I wish I was just sick and that I had just dreamed that Butterscotch was gone.* "I don't understand," she said finally. "Why did Jesus let Butterscotch run away again after I apologized to DeeDee like He wanted?"

"Jenny, look at me," her mother said sternly. Jenny lifted her head and looked directly at her mother. "Is that what you think? That Jesus was waiting for you to apologize to DeeDee before He sent Butterscotch back?"

Jenny nodded her head slowly. "Sort of."

"Honey, Jesus didn't expect you to apologize to DeeDee because you had to or so that He will do what you want Him to. He wanted you to apologize to DeeDee because you love Him and want to make Him happy. Do you understand?"

"I think so," Jenny said. But understanding didn't take away her sadness. That night, with the lights out, she stared out her window until her eyelids refused to stay open any longer.

In the Shoebox that week, all the kids were so excited about Family Day that no one really noticed how sad Jenny was. She sat in the back of the room watching everyone and wishing she could get excited about Family Day too.

Mrs. Shue told them about the booth that the Shoebox Kids would be running. "It's the 'Go Fish' booth," she said. She held up a broomstick with a string attached to it tied to a clothespin.

"The children will take one of these fishing poles and let the line down on the other side of the counter like this. Maria, come help me catch this prize." Maria ducked down behind the table. When Mrs. Shue tossed her fishing line over the counter, Maria took out a small prize and attached it to the clothespin. Then she tugged on the line, and Mrs. Shue pulled it up.

"See," Mrs. Shue said, holding up the prize, each child who plays will receive a prize like this one. It will cost fifty cents each time they 'Go Fish,' and the money that we earn will go to help pay for our camping trip at the end of the summer. We'll all take turns hiding behind the counter to attach the prizes so that everyone will have time to visit the other displays."

What if we don't want to visit the other displays? Jenny asked silently. *What if we don't want to come at all? Maybe I'll pretend I'm sick that day. No, Dad promised to come to Family Day, and I want to see him. I'm just going to have to try to have a little fun, even if I can't show Butterscotch in the pet show.* The thought made her sad again. *Oh, Butterscotch, where are you?*

She was still thinking the same thing when she went to sleep that night.

"Jenny."

Jenny sat straight up. "What? Oh, it's you, Mom." It took a few seconds to remember where she was and why she was clutching Butterscotch's battered old stuffed mouse. All she could remember was that Butterscotch was gone. Again. Probably forever.

"Honey? It's time to leave for Family Day," Mom said. "Natalie called and said she's ready to go."

Jenny put Butterscotch's old mouse on her dresser. *Now I remember—I fell asleep thinking about Butterscotch.* She sighed. *One thing is for sure—Butterscotch and I won't be entering the pet show today.*

Jenny tried to be happy as her friend got in the car. She didn't want to ruin Natalie's day. But, it was awfully hard being happy when she was sad and mad inside.

"Your father said he would be a little late," Jenny's mom told her as they pulled into the parking lot. "Why don't you take Natalie over to the Shoebox display and show her the hawk feather and hummingbird nest you found?"

Jenny led Natalie over to the Shoebox display and showed Natalie the things she'd found a few weeks ago on a nature hike. Out of the corner of her eye, she saw that the pet show was about to start.

"Do you want to watch?" Natalie asked.

"No . . . well, Yes," Jenny admitted.

Natalie took her by the arm and steered her over to a spot where they could see better. Dr. Givens, the veterinarian, was standing in the middle of a big circle of animals. He had on a long white lab coat and looked very important.

Jenny looked at all the animals. Chris Vargas was trying to keep his hamster, Herman, in a shoebox until Dr. Givens could look at him. Willie and his dog Coco were practicing some tricks while they waited to be judged. But Jenny's eyes stopped at Sammy and his cat Whispers.

She walked over closer and heard Whispers' quiet *meow! He sounds just like Butterscotch.* Jenny blinked quickly. *I don't want to start crying right here.*

"Whispers sure does look nice, don't you think?" a voice at Jenny's elbow asked.

Jenny swung around. Natalie was no longer beside her. Instead, she saw DeeDee and Tevin smiling at her as they munched on corndogs. Tevin watched the animals closely as if he was going to judge them.

"If it was up to me," Tevin said finally, "I'd choose Whispers."

"Well, it isn't up to you," Jenny snapped.

"Besides, it shouldn't be too hard for Whispers to win anyway, now that Butterscotch is gone. Maybe that's what you wanted in the first place. I hope you're happy!"

9

Going Fishing

With that, Jenny whirled around and pushed her way through the people crowded around to watch the pet show. She walked as fast as she could until she bumped headfirst into someone.

"Umphh!" the man groaned. "Jenny?!"

Jenny looked up slowly. It was her father and by the look on his face, Jenny could tell that he'd heard what she had said to Tevin. "Hi, Dad," she said softly. She tried to smile, but it felt as if her face might crack, so she gave up.

"Jenny, what just happened here?" Dad asked, as he took her arm and led her away from all the people. They walked over to where he'd parked his car, and he leaned up against the fender. "OK, tell me what's going on? Who is that with DeeDee? And why did you treat him so badly?"

"Because it's his fault!" Jenny burst out before she could help herself. "It's all his fault that Butterscotch disappeared. If it wasn't for his nasty dog, Butterscotch would be here right now, and we'd be taking home the blue ribbon. You should have seen her, Dad. I had her coat so shiny! And I spent an entire week studying everything there is to know about cats. Ask me a question. Any question."

Dad held up his hands. "Whoa! Slow down. First of all, I realize how disappointed you must be, Jenny, and how sad you are that Butterscotch is gone, but do you think that the way you're acting would make Jesus happy?"

Jenny was silent for a moment. *Of course not,* she thought. *Jesus would never have said that to Tevin. Jesus would have been friendly and happy. He would have introduced Natalie to DeeDee and Tevin. Then maybe they would have all watched the pet show together.*

"No," Jenny said slowly, her eyes studying the pavement. "No, I don't think the way I'm acting would make Jesus happy."

"Jenny," Dad said. "You need to forgive Tevin."

Jenny looked up, her eyes wide in surprise. "But, Dad, I already forgave Tevin. When he asked me to."

"Honey, when we forgive someone, we also forget what they did." He took Jenny by the shoulders and turned her around so that she was facing the Shoebox "Go Fish" booth. "The Bible says that Jesus took our sins and threw them into a big sea. And do you know what?"

Jenny shook her head.

Her father pointed to the little boy trying to get his fishing line to drop over the other side of the counter where Maria waited to attach his prize. "He tells us not to go fishing."

Jenny looked up at her father. "You mean that remembering what Tevin did is like fishing for the sin?"

Jenny's dad nodded. "Exactly. And Jesus doesn't want us to go fishing around with our old sins. He forgets about them, and we should too."

Dad bent down and looked in Jenny's eyes. "And, honey? That's what you need to do with Tevin."

"I will," Jenny promised.

Dad stood up and looked over at the pet show. "Look at that," he chuckled. "Sammy and Whispers have won the pet show. Why don't you go over and congratulate him?" he suggested. "And maybe while you're over there, you could apologize to Tevin."

Jenny looked over at Sammy, surrounded by people telling him what a good job he'd done. Right next to him was Tevin and DeeDee. *Yes,* she decided, *that's just what I'll do.*

"Thanks, Dad," Jenny said. "I will."

The next week in the Shoebox, everyone arrived early. They spent the time talking about Family Day. "Did you see Pastor Hill at the dunk tank?" Chris asked. "He really got wet."

As the other kids talked about their favorite parts, Jenny sat quietly in the back. Mrs. Shue came up behind her and laid her hands on Jenny's shoulders. "How are you doing today, Jenny?" she asked.

"Not as good as they are," Jenny said. Then she told Mrs. Shue about Butterscotch and everything.

"Your mother mentioned this," Mrs. Shue admitted. "But I didn't know that Butterscotch was found and then lost again. I'm sorry."

"I'm afraid I didn't act much like Jesus this week," Jenny said sadly.

"Oh, I don't know about that," Mrs. Shue said. "You are learning how to forgive people's 'debts,' or sins, against you the way Jesus forgives our 'debts,' or sins, against Him." She smiled brightly. "I think you're looking more and more like Jesus every day."

Jenny felt herself smile back. It was the first real smile that she could remember smiling since the day Butterscotch disappeared.

"Thanks, Mrs. Shue," she said.

"Can I have your attention, everyone?" Mrs. Shue asked as she walked to the front. "It's time to begin. Before we open this week's lesson, Can anyone remember what we learned last week?"

"We learned about the unforgiving servant," Willie said. "And about forgiveness."

Mrs. Shue nodded. "Did anyone give or experience forgiveness this week?"

Jenny wasn't sure she wanted to talk about Tevin and Butterscotch. Sammy spoke up first.

"I did," he said softly. Jenny leaned forward so that she could hear every word he said. Sammy looked around the Shoebox. "You know that my cat Whispers and I won a blue ribbon at the Family Day pet show. Well, I put it in a special box and set it on the kitchen table. My grandfather didn't know it was in there, and he threw it away by accident."

Jenny gasped. *He threw away the beautiful blue ribbon!* Jenny thought about the bare space on her own wall at home. *I know how Sammy must feel. Awful!*

"Grandfather asked me to forgive him," Sammy continued. "At first I didn't feel as if I could. But he didn't mean to throw the ribbon away. It was an accident. I told Grandfather that I forgave him, but I was still angry with him. Then I said a prayer to Jesus to take the angry feeling away and help me to really forgive Grandfather as the king forgave the servant." Sammy looked around the room. "And He did."

That made Jenny think hard, especially about Tevin. *I need to do what Sammy did,* she decided. "Dear Jesus," she prayed silently, "please help me to feel real forgiveness toward Tevin, even though he tried to take Butterscotch away. Amen."

When their lesson was over, Jenny sat in her chair thinking. *What if I took one of my blue hair ribbons—maybe that really pretty one I found in the garage—and a gold belt buckle, and made a blue ribbon? Maybe with a little glue and some help from Mom, it would be nice enough to give to Sammy to replace his lost one!*

The more she thought about it, the more excited she got. *Won't Sammy be surprised?*

As Jenny searched for the ribbon at home that night, she packed up the last of Butterscotch's old battered toys into a cardboard box and carried them to the hall closet. *If I put them in here, they will be less likely to remind me of Butterscotch. Maybe I should throw them away. What if . . . someday . . . I decide to get a kitten? A kitten would probably enjoy playing with the toys as much as Butterscotch had.*

Jenny held the box above her head and strained to reach the top shelf of the closet. Before she managed to push it up there, she heard a strange sound. It sounded like . . . "meow."

Jenny shook her head fiercely. *It's bad enough that I dream about Butterscotch all the time; now I'm starting to hear her too.* She walked back into her room.

Blam! Something hit the screen on her window like a rock.

10

More Than Butterscotch

"Mom!" Jenny shouted. "Something's outside my window. Or someone. Mom?"

As soon as her mother got there, they both tiptoed over to the window and peeked out. "I don't see anything," Mom said. She reached up and pulled the window closed. Then she shut the curtains.

"Should we go outside and look?" Jenny asked.

"Maybe. Let's go turn on the porch light and look around." When they didn't see anything through the peephole in the door, Mrs. Wallace turned the doorknob and opened it just enough to stick her head out.

Just enough for something to run in.

Meow!

"Butterscotch?" Jenny couldn't believe her eyes, even as her cat wove around and around her legs, purring loudly.

"Butterscotch!" Jenny whooped. "Oh, Butterscotch, I missed you so much!" Jenny picked up her cat and buried her face in the soft fur.

Mrs. Wallace rubbed Butterscotch's head and smiled. "Oh, Jenny, I'm so glad she came back."

It didn't take much talking to convince Jenny's mom that since Butterscotch had come back, she needed a new cat bed and some new toys. All her toys were so old and shabby.

Jenny's mom laughed. "I suppose nothing will be too good for that cat now."

That evening, Jenny had a hard time going to sleep again. But this time it was because she was so happy. "Thank You, God," she whispered as Butterscotch purred beside her.

"Oh no!" Jenny said the next morning as Butterscotch ate her special cat food. "I forgot to tell Natalie! Can I call her?"

"Finish eating first," her mom answered.

Jenny finished quickly and picked up the phone while Butterscotch kept eating.

"Natalie? Come over as soon as you can. I've got something to show you."

Jenny was ready when the doorbell rang. "Look who's home!" she shouted as she opened the door with Butterscotch on her shoulder.

"She came back!" Natalie squealed. "I'm so happy for you, Jenny."

"Thanks for helping me find her," Jenny said. "Do you want to hold her?"

Natalie petted the purring cat, then got a surprised look on her face. "Someone must have been feeding her. Feel how fat she is."

Jenny reached over to feel. "You know, I thought she would be skinny too. She's really fat." Then a panicked look came over her face. "What if it's not fat? What if something's wrong with her?"

Grabbing the cat, she raced out to the living room. Natalie was right behind her. She dumped the cat onto her mother's lap, tears streaming down her face. "Mom, I think Butterscotch has a tumor. Feel her stomach."

Mrs. Wallace pushed and poked Butterscotch's stomach. Then she smiled. "Jenny, Butterscotch doesn't have a tumor. She's going to have kittens."

"Kittens?" Jenny asked blankly.

"Kittens!" Natalie shrieked. "Can I have one?"

"Yes, if it's OK with your parents. We won't be able to keep any," Mrs. Wallace said.

"We won't?" Jenny asked. "Why not?"

"We can't feed another cat, Jenny," her mother said firmly, and Jenny knew there was no use arguing. She looked sadly at Butterscotch. How could she give away her kittens?

Later, after Natalie had gone home and Butterscotch was curled up at the foot of Jenny's bed, Jenny sat down beside her mother on the couch. "Mom, why can't we keep the kittens?" she began. "They won't be any trouble. Honest. I'll do everything to take care of them. You won't have to do a thing."

Mom sighed and put down the magazine she was reading. "I'm sorry, Jenny, but we can't have a bunch of cats running around here."

"But," Jenny pouted, "you said I could have a kitten."

Mom smiled. "That was before Butterscotch came back."

"It's all Tevin's fault," she grumped, then as

she realized what she'd said, her hand flew to cover her mouth. "Oops, I guess I just went 'fishing,' " she said.

"You know, Jenny, you keep blaming Tevin because Butterscotch ran away, but I remember that night a little differently than you." Jenny squirmed uncomfortably on the sofa. "I remember a certain girl who was asked twice to bring her cat inside. Do you remember who that girl was?"

Jenny swallowed hard. "Me?" she squeaked.

Mom nodded. "Could Shorty have chased Butterscotch away if she was safe inside where she belonged?"

"No," Jenny said in a small voice. "It was really my fault that Butterscotch ran away, wasn't it?" she asked.

Jenny didn't need to see her mother nod to know it was true. "I'm sorry, Mom. Will you forgive me?" Mom threw her arms around Jenny and hugged her tight. Jenny hugged back as hard as she could. "And remember, Mom, no fishing!"

Though Jenny thought Butterscotch's kittens would never arrive, one day when she got home from school, Butterscotch cuddled with three tiny little kittens.

Jenny's fingers itched to hold those furry little kittens. Finally, her mother said it was OK. She touched their soft fur. She "oohed" over their little paws. She "aahed" over their tiny tails. And then she had to decide whom to give them to.

Natalie was an easy first choice. She wanted the gold-and-white tiger. "I'm going to call him Garfield."

Tevin's parents called to see how Butterscotch was, and when they heard about the kittens, they asked for one. Tevin wanted the one that looked the most like Butterscotch, so Jenny decided to give him the yellow one. The white one with the yellow rings on its tail went to Mrs. Norton's niece.

DeeDee came over to play the day that Tevin's dad was supposed to stop by for the kitten. She brought a ball of her mother's yarn, and they squealed with delight as the kitten chased it around the living room.

Soon Tevin's dad pulled up in the driveway, and the girls brought the kitten out to him. Jenny gave him the big box that she and DeeDee had poked holes in. "He can ride in this," she said. "And here's a few of Butterscotch's old toys to keep him happy."

"Thank you very much, girls," Mr. Ryan said. He scratched the kitten under the chin. "Tevin's really going to like this little guy. I'm not sure about Shorty, though!"

"They'll learn to love each other," Jenny promised.

"When is Butterscotch going to have more kittens?" DeeDee asked as they watched Mr. Ryan back out of the driveway.

"Never," Jenny said. "She has an appointment with Dr. Givens, the veterinarian, so that she won't ever have kittens again." She sighed. "I guess it's a good thing. It's too hard giving kittens away, even when you know they're going to good homes."

"So what do you want to play?" DeeDee asked.

"Let's go down to Natalie's house," Jenny suggested. They started across the yard, then Jenny stopped. "Wait! I'm going to make sure Butterscotch is inside. I don't want her getting cat-napped again."